The Computer Munched My Homework and Other Classroom Jokes

by Dianne Woo

Illustrated by Jack White

TOR ®

A TOM DOHERTY ASSOCIATES BOOK
NEW YORK

This is a work of fiction. All the characters and eventsportrayed in this book are fictitious, and any resemblance to real people or events is purely coincidental.

THE COMPUTER MUNCHED MY HOMEWORK AND OTHER CLASSROOM JOKES

Cover and interior art by Jack White

A Tor Book
Published by Tom Doherty Associates, Inc.
175 Fifth Avenue
New York, N.Y. 10010

Tor® is a registered trademark of Tom Doherty Associates, Inc.

ISBN 0-812-52050-5

First edition: September 1992

Printed in the United States of America

0 9 8 7 6 5 4 3 2 1

Student: Teacher, may I leave the class?
Teacher: Well, you certainly can't take it with
you.

How do the cooks know there's enough bread in the school cafeteria?
They take a roll call.

What did the principal say when she got a call from Mr. Hamm and a call from the mayor at the same time?
"I'll have the Hamm, hold the mayor."

Billie: It hurts to hold my head up. I'd better go
see the nurse.
Millie: Neck's weak?
Billie: No, I need to go right now!

What do you call the head of a fish school?
The sar-dean. *(sardine)*

Why do oysters do so well in school?
Because they have pearls of wisdom.

1

What do yuppie rabbits become after they finish business school?
Million-hares.

Teacher: Please help Cindy. She was playing
the harmonica, and she swallowed it!
Nurse: I'm glad she wasn't playing the piano.

Student: Nurse, I feel like a deck of cards.
Nurse: Hold on, I'll deal with you later.

Teacher: Who can tell me what kind of animal
    life there is in Paris?
Joey: Rabbits. They're in the hutch—back of
    Notre Dame.

*Why did the band teacher hire tutors for her
students?*
    She thought they needed band-aids.

What's yellow and plays in the school orchestra?
    A band-ana.

Teacher: Class, who can tell me why Robin
    Hood and Maid Marian lived happily ever
    after?
Student: Because Robin heard what made
    marryin' great.

Maggie: Why are you carrying that rabbit's foot?
Mark: It's for good luck. I'm scared to death of
    tests.
Maggie: But we don't have a test today.
Mark: See! It's working!

What happened when the forgetful choir director found the door to his office locked?
   He knew he needed to find the right key.

What's an ancient-history teacher's favorite TV show?
   "Name That Tomb."

What's yellow outside, black and white inside, and very crowded?
   A school bus full of zebras.

Did you hear about the soccer team that kept stumbling during their first game?
   It was a real field trip.

Why is the head cook in the school cafeteria so mean?
   Because he beats the eggs.

Coach: Did you do your exercises this morning?
Student: Yes, ma'am. I bent over and touched my shoes a hundred times.
Coach: Good! What did you do next?
Student: I took the shoes off the chair and put them on my feet.

What's a cheerleader's favorite flavor of ice cream?
· Rahs-berry.

Why did the chicken cross the playground?
To get to the other slide.

Student: Nurse, I feel like a dog.
Nurse: Sit!

What's the difference between one classroom and two classrooms?
Usually a wall.

How do you tell the difference between a person who is late for a train and a teacher in a girl's school?
One misses the train, the other trains the misses.

When do 3 and 3 make more than 6?
When they make 33.

Mother: How were the crackers in your lunch today, Jimmy?
Jimmy: Crummy.

What song do custodians like best?
    "Singin' in the Drain."

What never went to school but can speak every language?
    An echo.

Lizzie: I forgot everything I learned in school today.
Mother: Well, what do you know?

*What did the home economics teacher say
when he dropped an egg on his foot?*
   "The yolk's on me."

Teacher: Why were the Middle Ages called the
      Dark Ages?
Casey: Because there were so many knights.

How can three ones equal two?
   $1 + \frac{1}{1} = 2.$

How many times can you subtract 2 from 10?
   Just one time, because after you subtract it
   once, you no longer have 10.

Teacher: Class, who can tell me what country
      needs the most food?
Student: Hungary.

What's the difference between 10 and 100?
   Zero. (0)

Teacher: Class, what country is popular on
      Thanksgiving Day?
Student: Turkey.

Where did the cooking teacher go on vacation?
  Greece. *(grease)*

Teacher: What did Paul Revere say when he
    finished his famous ride?
Zoey: "Whoa!"

Why are the best students always on the run?
  Because they are pursuing their studies.

Tim: "Tammy taught the tiny tots to talk." How
    many T's are there in that?
Mike: There are only two T's in "that."

What vowel makes the most noise?
  An O, because all the other vowels are in-
  audible. *(in the word "audible")*

What kind of test does a spelling teacher give?
  N–X–M.

Kerry: My sister is really smart. She can spell her
    name backwards, and she's only in the first
    grade.
Harry: That's great! What's her name?
Kerry: Hannah.

Cal: The brain is a wonderful invention, but I can't figure it out.

Hal: What makes you say that?

Cal: Well, it starts working the minute you get up in the morning and never stops until the moment the teacher calls on you in class.

What two siblings were never wrong?
   The Wright Brothers.

Teacher: If you worked for ten hours at a wage
     of one dollar per hour what would you get?
Student: A new job.

*What do the classroom, the playground, and
baseball have in common?*
     They all have slides.

Father: Did you take an art class today?
Son: No, why? Is there one missing?

Teacher: Sally, what is 6 plus 7?
Sally: I don't know, I only have 10 fingers.

What did the acorn say when she grew up?
     "Gee-om-a-tree!" *(Geometry)*

What kind of cars do government officials drive?
     Civics.

Where does Rambo work out?
     On the jungle gym.

Why did Suzy jog while studying for her test?
     She wanted to get a physical education.

What do you say to your spelling teacher when she slips on the ice?
    R–U–O–K?

Teacher: If a Russian ruler is called a czar, and his wife is called a czarina, what are his children called?
Student: Czardines?

What do Santa's children carry in their lunch boxes?
    Ho-Ho's.

Ellen: Hey, I found 50 cents in front of school today!

Helen: Oh, that's mine. I dropped a half-dollar there this morning.

Ellen: But I found two quarters!

Helen: Well, it probably broke when it hit the pavement.

What piece of playground equipment taught the girl after school?
Tutor-totter. *(Tutor taught her)*

What did the pencil say to the eraser?
Nothing. Pencils can't talk.

How can you get a female dog to do new tricks?
Teacher. *(teach her)*

What happens when kids go to school year-round?
Some aren't on vacation and summer. *(some are)*

What did the eye doctor say to the teacher?
"Your pupils need classes."

Teacher: How well do you like art?
Student: I don't know, I've never even met him.

What's a music teacher's favorite animal?
  A horned toad.

What did the spelling teacher say to the gorilla?
  U–R–N–N–M–L.

Teacher: Who can tell me what Camelot was
        famous for?
Sam: Its knight-life!

What's a geography teacher's favorite food?
  Eskimo pies.

What food do gym teachers like best?
  Bar-bell-cue ribs.

Principal: Well, young man, this is the fifth
        straight day you've been late to class. Have
        you anything to say for yourself?
Student: Boy, am I glad it's Friday!

13

Where's a gym teacher's favorite place to visit?
  The Golf of Mexico.

What's a gym teacher's favorite TV show?
  "Star Track."

What food do music teachers like best?
  Drumsticks.

What did the spelling teacher say after a long, hard day?
  I–M–C–P.

Why is riding a bike over barbed wire like a music lesson?
  You get sharps and flats.

Larry: Psst! How long did the War of 1812 last?
Mary: One year, then it became the War of 1813.

What do you say when your library book is overdue?
  "Fine!"

14

What kind of sandwich gets all the attention in the cafeteria?
A ham sandwich.

What's green and white, and scared when you open your lunch box?
A chicken salad sandwich.

What snack is like the school bell?
Ding Dongs.

Jenny: My sandwich is bigger than your salami
    sandwich.
Benny: That's baloney!
Jenny: You're right.

What did the bread say to the muffin?
  "Meet me behind the school cafeteria and
  we'll e-loaf." *(elope)*

*What do you get when you cross a building of
education with a boxer who's been knocked
out?*
  School daze.

What did the pencil say to the eraser?
  "Get the lead out."

Willy: Teacher, I know a company in Asia which
    makes writing liquid.
Teacher: Oh, yes? What is it called?
Willy: India, Inc. *(ink)*

*What happened when the computer was late to
the school cafeteria?*
  He couldn't get a byte.

16

What did the ruler say to the compass when they got into a fight?
  "I get the point! Let it slide!"

What's a wood-shop teacher's favorite food?
  Chipped beef.

What's a wood-shop teacher's favorite science-fiction film?
  "Saw Wars."

Father: I heard you played hooky from school today and played baseball with your friends.
Son: No, Dad, and I have the fish to prove it!

Why did the computer and the disk fight over the car?
  Because the computer wouldn't let the disk drive.

Math teacher: Henry, how many feet are in a yard?
Henry: Depends how many people are in it.

17

Why did the music teacher get glasses?
So he could C-sharp.

Librarian: Shh! Can't you kids see the sign? It says "Silence!"
Student: We were just giving each other some sound advice.

What did the eraser do when she fought with the pencil?
She rubbed him out.

Why did the drama student leap forward when she saw another student actor tumble off the stage?
She wanted to catch a falling star.

Todd: I tell the best riddles in school!
Rod: You must be joke-King. *(joking)*

What is a fruit's favorite subject?
Currant events.

How do you make a slide rule?
Give him a crown, a robe, and a scepter.

18

When is a school bus not a school bus?
  When it turns into a parking lot.

Nurse: Let me take your temperature.
Student: No way! It's the only one I've got!

Did you hear the joke about the broken pencil?
  There's no point to it.

Bill: My teacher must really like me.
Gil: What makes you say that?
Bill: She's kept me in her class four years in a
  row.

What's a baseball coach's motto?
  "If at first you don't succeed, try for second."

Tammy: Our class has to sing all of "America
  the Beautiful" every single day! It takes too
  much time.
Sammy: You're lucky. We have to sing the
  "Stars and Stripes" forever!

What's black and white and red all over?
  A textbook.

19

Teacher: Who was the Englishman who built up
the British navy?
Student: Sir Launch-a-lot.

What do you call the study of famous women?
Herstory.

Bertha: Somebody stole all the pastries out of
the cafeteria!
Bella: Well, doesn't that take the cake!

*What's the difference between a dog with fleas
and a bored student?*
One is going to itch, the other is itching to go.

*What's the difference between an obedient dog
and a disobedient student?*
One rarely bites, the other barely writes.

John: Teacher, I know who built the first
airplane that *didn't* fly.
Teacher: Who was that?
John: The Wrong Brothers.

What's the first thing an ape learns in school?
The Ape–B–C's.

Why did the letter E flunk?
It was always in bed and never in school.

Chemistry teacher: Who can tell me the formula
    for water?
Student: H, I, J, K, L, M, N, O.
Teacher: That's not correct.
Student: I thought you said that formula was H
    to O.

A mother was talking to the school psychologist about her son. "I'm worried about him. He thinks he's a monkey. All day long he swings from trees."

The psychologist told her, "Don't worry, ma'am. I'm sure it's just a phase. He'll grow out of it."

The mother looked relieved. "Oh, thank you, doctor. How much do I owe you?"

"Forty bananas," the doctor replied.

Teacher: What do you get when you divide 327,910 by 3?
Student: The wrong answer.

How did the astronaut's daughter pack her food?
In a launch box.

What do you do when your computer wants a snack?
Feed it microchips.

What do music teachers drink when they're thirsty?
Root-beer flutes.

What does a class of monkeys sing?
  "The Star-Spangled Banana."

What seafood do gym coaches like best?
  Mussels. *(muscles)*

History teacher: Class, did you know John Paul
    Jones was famous for saying, "I have not
    yet begun to fight!"?
Student: No wonder his side lost!

How is a bad riddle like an unsharpened pencil?
  It has no point.

An absent-minded principal arrived home in
the evening after working late at school. When
he got to the door of his house, he realized he
had forgotten his key. He knocked on the door.
  His wife looked out the peephole, but it was
so dark that she didn't recognize him. "I'm
sorry, sir," she said, "but my husband isn't
home yet."
  The absent-minded principal thought a
moment, then said, "All right, I'll come back
tomorrow."

Teacher: What are you painting, Mary?
Mary: It's a picture of a cow eating grass.
Teacher: Where is the grass?
Mary: The cow ate it.
Teacher: But where is the cow?
Mary: Well, why would he hang around if all the
grass is gone?

*What has stripes and sits at the head of the
class?*
  The flag.

Teacher: I can hardly read your handwriting.
    You must try to write more clearly.
Timmy: If I did that, then you'd complain about
    my spelling.

Where can a student find money easily?
  In the dictionary.

Why can't elephants go to college?
  Because most can't graduate from high
  school.

Who wrote the Bad Student's Handbook?
  I. M. Lazee.

Barb: Teacher, I think there's a rabbit in my computer.

Teacher: Good heavens! What makes you say that?

Barb: I keep getting floppy disks.

What do you call a teacher who shouts?
  A loud speaker.

Candy: On our field trip to the farm we saw a hen that laid an egg five inches long. Can you beat that?

Sandy: Yes, with an eggbeater.

Millie: When I grow up, I want to be a vitamin.

Jillie: Don't be silly. You can't be a vitamin.

Millie: Yes, I can. I saw a sign in a store window that said "Vitamin B-1."

What resembles half of a basketball?
  The other half.

Teacher: What is the hardest thing for you in school?

Student: Whispering to my friend without moving my lips.

Why couldn't Joey take tennis lessons after school?
  His mother didn't want him to raise a racket.

Principal: Did you see which way the computer went?

Student: Data way! *(that a way)*

Teacher: Did you think the test questions were hard?

Student: No, the questions were easy. It was the answers that were hard.

What subject do cows like best?
  Moo-sic.

Student: I wish I had been born a hundred
    years ago.
History teacher: Why?
Student: Because I'd have one hundred less
    years of history to study.

Geography teacher: Where are the Great
    Plains?
Student: At the airport.

Why do birds hang around libraries?
  To catch bookworms.

Teacher: What is the most important thing to
    remember in chemistry class?
Student: Don't lick the spoon.

What subject do bees like best?
  Buzz-ness. *(business)*

English teacher: What is an autobiography?
Student: A book about a car's life.

What does your spelling teacher get when she rides the merry-go-round too many times?
  D–Z.

Geography teacher: Where can we find fjords?
Student: In the parking lot.

What do you get when you cross a math teacher with a crab?
  Snappy answers.

Teacher: Why will TV never replace the
    newspaper?
Student: You can't swat flies with a TV.

What do you call the back door of the cafeteria?
  The bacteria.

Driving instructor: Why isn't it a good idea to
    use snow tires in the summer?
Student: They might melt.

If there is a head of the class and a bottom of the class, what's in between?
  The student body.

Student: I didn't deserve a zero on this paper!
Teacher: I know, but it was the lowest grade I
could give you.

Principal: Are you trying to tell me that your
teacher yelled at you for something you
didn't do?
Student: Yes, my homework.

Why are fish so smart?
They hang out in schools.

Mother: Your teacher said you're at the bottom of your class.
Student: That's OK, we learn the same at both ends.

Which insect is the smartest?
The spelling bee.

Science teacher: Which bird is smarter, the owl or the chicken?
Student: The owl.
Teacher: How do we know?
Student: Have you ever eaten Kentucky Fried Owl?

Why is one foot greater than three feet?
One foot makes a ruler.

Geography teacher: Open your books to page 14. Who can tell me where Rome is?
Student: On page 15.

Student: I'll be home sick tomorrow.
Teacher: I didn't know you were feeling ill.
Student: I'm not now, but I will be after my dad sees my report card.

What do you feed a hungry cheerleading squad?
    Cheer-ios!

Why do math teachers dice their carrots?
    They like square roots.

What did the tall teacher say to the short student?
    "Speak up when you talk to me."

Student: I'm not going to Spanish class today.
Teacher: Why not?
Student: My throat hurts and I can barely speak
    English.

What's a teacher's favorite nation?
    Expla-nation.

Teacher: I hope I didn't see you looking at your
    neighbor's paper.
Student: I hope you didn't either.

Gym teacher: What's the hardest thing about
    learning to walk the balance beam?
Student: The gym floor.

31

What's a science teacher's favorite TV show?
   "Whale of Fortune."

Father: Do you have anything positive to say
      about my son?
Teacher: Yes, with grades like these he certainly
      can't be cheating.

*What did the track coach say after a long, hard
day?*
   "I can't wait to run a bath."

Dance instructor: There are two things that can
      keep anyone from being a good dancer.
      Do you know what they are?
Student: Yes, one's feet.

What's a music teacher's favorite food?
   Minuet rice.

Mother: How do you like your new school?
Student: Closed!

What word is very smart, yet dumb?
   Wis-dumb. *(wisdom)*

32

Teacher: Where is Moscow located?
Student: In the barn with Pa's cow.

What's in the middle of every class?
  The letter A.

What letter is not found in the alphabet?
  The kind you mail.

Science teacher: How can we get the mercury
  to go up and down?
Student: Put it in an elevator.

*When is a classroom like two letters of the
alphabet?*
  When it is M–T. *(empty)*

Principal: I thought I told you never to walk into
  school late again!
Student: I know, that's why I'm running.

*Why shouldn't a Chinese-food chef play pitcher
in a baseball game?*
  Because he woks everyone.

Teacher: I'd like to go one day without giving
  you detention!
Student: OK, how about today?

What plays hangman and flies?
  A spelling bee.

Why are textbooks and tall buildings alike?
  They both contain many stories.

Music teacher: What's an operetta?
Student: Someone who works for the phone
    company.

*What word is usually pronounced wrong by
teachers?*
    Wrong.

History teacher: Which leader do you think
    made the biggest mistake in history?
Student: Noah. He should have swatted both
    flies when he had a chance.

Teacher: I don't want you talking in class
    anymore!
Student: That's OK. I don't need to talk any
    more, I'm talking enough already.

Music teacher: Why are you banging the side of
    your head on the piano?
Student: I'm playing by ear.

Math teacher: If I had five cows and ten goats,
    what would I have?
Student: Plenty of milk.

What's furry, barks, and loves school?
  A teacher's pet.

Student: Mom, will you do my homework?
Mother: No, it wouldn't be right.
Student: That's OK, as long as you just do your
      best.

What question must a student always answer
with "yes"?
  "What does Y–E–S spell?"

History teacher: What do George Washington and Abraham Lincoln have in common?
Student: They're both dead.

How can eight 8's be added to make 1,000?
888 + 88 + 8 + 8 + 8 = 1,000.

First student: A, B, C, D, E, F, G. What comes next?
Second student: Whiz!

What do you call two students coming on campus after hours?
A pair of sneakers.

Teacher: Where was Queen Elizabeth crowned?
Student: On her head.

Where do carpenters study?
Boarding school.

Principal: Your teacher said that you missed school yesterday.
Student: No, I was so busy fishing, I didn't miss school at all!

Why are eye doctors good teachers?
    They know how to treat pupils.

Geography teacher: What is the first thing you
        think of when I say Greece?
Student: My bicycle chain!

History teacher: Where was the Declaration of
        Independence signed?
Student: At the bottom.

*Why did the teacher prefer to have 30 students
instead of 20?*
    He wanted to have more class.

Teacher: Why does Billy run all the way home
        every day after school?
Student: He's trying to break Babe Ruth's
    consecutive home-run record.

Teacher: Are you having trouble hearing?
Student: No, I'm having trouble listening.

Which teacher wears the largest hat?
    The one with the largest head.

What's a witch's favorite subject?
  Spelling.

39

What was the computer's medical diagnosis?
  Terminal.

Teacher: Which month has 28 days?
Student: All of them do.

Which is easier to spell, "eat" or "feed"?
  "Feed" is spelled with more ease. *(E's)*

School counselor: I would suggest you enroll in
      night school.
Student: Oh no, I couldn't do that! I can't read
      in the dark.

*Why did the student bring a pair of scissors to
school?*
  She wanted to cut class.

Student: Mom, I can't take any more baths.
Mother: Why not?
Student: My teacher said that if I get into hot
      water again, I'll be expelled.

Can pencils start anything?
  No, they can only be lead.

40

Mother: My son said that he got 100 on all his
tests.
Teacher: He did—25 in spelling, 25 in math, 25
in history, and 25 in science.

Why do soccer players get the best grades?
Because they use their heads.

Teacher: Here's your report card.
Student: I don't want to scare you, but my dad
said that if this report card is bad, the
person responsible is going to be spanked!

*What do you call a computer that hasn't been
used for a long time?*
Key-bored. *(keyboard)*

Teacher: This is the fifth time this week you've
been late. What do you think I should do
about it?
Student: Don't wait.

Student: I think my teacher is dumb.
Father: Why do you think that?
Student: He's always asking the class questions.

Teacher: How did people entertain themselves
    in the Middle Ages?
Student: They went to knight-clubs.

Where does a track star wash her shoes?
    Under running water.

Teacher: Do you know what this "F" on your homework means?
Student: "Fantastic"?

Father: What did you learn in school today?
Student: Writing.
Father: What did you write?
Student: I don't know, we haven't learned to read yet.

Student: I'm having a hard time learning how to spell.
Teacher: Why?
Student: Because all the words are different.

Teacher: Did you throw this rock through my classroom window?
Student: Yes, but it wasn't my fault.
Teacher: Whose fault was it?
Student: Johnny's—he ducked.

Math teacher: If I gave you one dollar each week for a whole year, what would you have?
Student: A new bike.

Teacher: Why is your essay about your pet exactly the same as your sister's?
Student: We have the same pet.

Teacher: Did your mother help you with your homework?
Student: No, she did it all by herself.

Teacher: Can you give me Lincoln's Gettysburg Address?
Student: I thought he lived in the White House.

Teacher: Why did you get such a low score on today's test?
Student: The girl who sits next to me is absent.

Teacher: The test time is almost up. How far are you from getting the correct answers?
Student: Two desks away.

What's the difference between a teacher and a train engineer?
A teacher trains minds, an engineer minds trains.

Student: My new school is haunted.
Mother: How do you know?
Student: My teacher is always talking about
school spirit.

Bus driver: Do you want to go to the junior high school or the senior high school?
Student: Neither, but I have to.

Student: I ain't got a pencil.
Teacher: I *haven't* got a pencil.
Student: That makes two of us.

Teacher: What do you think you'll be when you get out of school?
Student: Old!

Band director: Do you know how to clean your tuba?
Student: With a tuba toothpaste?

Math teacher: What's the difference between 2 and 5?
Student: The five is upside-down.

Student: My teacher can't make up her mind.
Mother: What do you mean?
Student: First she says that 2 and 2 is 4, and then she says that 3 and 1 are 4!

*How would you feel if you were kept after
school for failing the spelling test?*
  Spellbound.

Teacher: Can anyone tell me one thing that
    cowhide is used for?
Student: To hold the cow together.

Teacher: Did you study for this exam?
Student: Yes, I spent 8 hours on my book last
    night.
Teacher: Really?
Student: Yes, I fell asleep studying and slept on
    it all night.

Teacher: Do you know what the center of
    gravity is?
Student: "V."

What food do drama teachers like best?
  Ham.

Teacher: What is the plural of child?
Student: Twins.

47

What do spelling teachers eat for lunch?
  Alphabet soup.

Keith: How many sheep does it take to make one wool sweater?
Kathy: Gee, I didn't even know sheep could knit.

Teacher: If you study hard, you'll get ahead.
Student: No thanks, I already have a head.

Principal: Why are you running down the hall with that book in your hands?
Student: I'm speed-reading.

What is a snake's favorite subject?
  Hiss-tory.

Mother: Why did you get a zero on this homework assignment?
Student: That's not a zero. The teacher ran out of stars so she gave me a moon.

Teacher: Where is the English channel?
Student: I don't know, we don't get cable.

48

Lonnie: When I grow up, I want to be an Olympic athlete and a brilliant computer scientist.
Ronnie: Really? At the same time?
Lonnie: Yes, I'll be a floppy-discus thrower.

Grandmother: Do you like going to school?
Student: Yes, I like going and coming, but not the in-between part.

Student: I don't like history class.
Mother: Why not?
Student: Because my teacher keeps asking me about things that happened before I was born!

Teacher: I'm going to have to write a letter to your parents about this poor essay.
Student: I wouldn't do that.
Teacher: Why not?
Student: They wrote it.

How does a math teacher fix a leaky faucet?
   With multi-pliers.

Why are history teachers never lonely?
   They know a lot of dates.

Teacher: If I lay two eggs here, and three eggs here, how many eggs will there be?
Student: None. I don't believe you can lay eggs.

If a fish took a foreign language class, what would it be?
   Finn-ish.

Teacher: How do we know that George Washington was a general and not an admiral?
Student: An admiral would have known better than to stand up in a boat.

Why did the vampire take a typing course?
    He wanted to learn different blood types.

Why do you have to buy school supplies every year?
    Because you can't get them for free.

Teacher: Name one animal that we get fur from.
Student: Skunks.
Teacher: Are you sure?
Student: Yup! My daddy says that if I see a
skunk I "shud git as fur from it" as I kin!

Where did Sir Lancelot get his education?
Knight school.

Student: I'm going to be an astronaut and fly to
the sun.
Teacher: You can't fly to the sun—it's too hot.
Student: Then I'll go at night.

First child: Want to play school?
Second child: Only if I can be absent.

History teacher: Who said, "Give me liberty or
give me death?"
Student: Someone in detention.

Why did the rabbit get an "A" in math?
She was good at multiplication.

How do you spell jealousy?
I–N–V–U.

Astronomy teacher: What do we call a star with
a tail?
Student: Mickey Mouse.

Teacher: Can you define ignorance?
Student: I don't know what that means.
Teacher: That's correct.

Teacher: If you put your hand in your pocket
and found 2 quarters, 6 nickels, and a
dime, what would you have?
Student: Someone else's pants on!

Shop teacher: You hammer nails like lightning.
Student: You mean I'm very fast?
Shop teacher: No, you never strike twice in the
same place.

Teacher: Any 8-year-old should be able to do
these math problems.
Mother: Oh, well, no wonder my son can't do
them. He's 12.

Father: What kind of marks are you getting in
gym class?
Student: Bruises.

How do you make children grow?
  Put them in a kinder-garden.

What piece of furniture is good at math?
  A multiplication table.

First student: Do you believe in telling the future in cards?

Second student: Yes, I can take one look at my report card and know what my father will do when I get home.

How do you spell conceited?
   I–M–B–4–U.

How do bees get to school?
   They take a school buzz. *(bus)*

Teacher: I'm going to have to ask your mother to visit me.

Student: You'll be sorry.

Teacher: Why?

Student: My mother is a doctor and she charges $100 for a visit.

What word contains 26 letters but has only three syllables?
   Alphabet.

What teacher is always getting things wrong?
   Miss Take. *(mistake)*

55

Teacher: What do you get when you cut a
tomato into two parts?
Student: Halves.
Teacher: Into four parts?
Student: Quarters.
Teacher: What do you get when you cut the
quarters in half?
Student: Eighths.
Teacher: And what do you get when you cut
the eighths in half?
Student: Diced tomatoes.

Why are math teachers always sad?
  They have so many problems.

Mother: What did your teacher say when you
told her you were an only child?
Student: She said, "Thank goodness!"

Why is cabbage the smartest vegetable?
  It has a head.

Teacher: Today we're going to talk about the
shape that our world is in.
Student: We already know that it's round!

Where did the skating teacher go on vacation?
Iceland.

Why do owls do well in school?
    They give a hoot!

Teacher: Has anyone ever heard the term
    "financial genius"?
Student: Yes, my mother said that it is someone
    who can make money faster than I spend
    it.

How do you spell flirtatious?
    U–R–A–Q–T.

Teacher: Why are you running?
Student: I'm running to stop a fight.
Teacher: Who is fighting?
Student: Me and the guy chasing me.

First student: Would you be scared if you saw a
    man-eating lion?
Second student: No.
First student: Why not?
Second student: I'm a girl!

What happens to bad eggs at school?
    They get eggs-spelled. *(expelled)*

Teacher: Why did you keep pulling your tongue
    out of your mouth during the test?
Student: The answers were on the tip of my
    tongue.

Mother: What did you learn about in math class
    today?
Student: A couple of trees.
Mother: Trees?
Student: Yes, gee-om-uh-tree and trig-o-nom-
    uh-tree.

Why don't math teachers fear crime?
    There's safety in numbers.

Teacher: Why did you push your bike all the
    way to school today?
Student: I was so late I didn't have time to get
    on it.

Why is arithmetic tiring?
    You have to carry so many numbers.

What did the teacher say to the clock?
    "Quit tocking in my class!"

Why did the music teacher bring ladders to class?
He wanted his students to sing higher.

How do computers eat?
  In megabytes.

What does a skeleton do before a big exam?
  He bones up on things.

Teacher: You have 10 fingers. If you had four
    less, what would you have?
Student: No more piano lessons!

Why did the biology student get expelled?
  He got caught counting his ribs during an
  exam.

Teacher: Robert Burns wrote "To a Field
    Mouse."
Student: I bet the mouse never replied!

Teacher: If I had four oranges in this hand and
    ten apples in this hand, what would I have?
Student: Big hands!

*What do you get when you cross a dog with a
piano teacher?*
  A dog whose Bach is worse than its bite.

School nurse: You look tired.
Student: I am. I was up all night studying for my
    blood test.

Mother: How do you know my son was
    cheating?
Teacher: His answers are exactly the same as
    the boy who sits next to him, except for
    one.
Mother: Well, if that one answer is different, isn't
    it possible that this is just a coincidence?
Teacher: I don't think so. The other boy's
    answer was, "I don't know." Your son's
    answer was, "Me neither."

Teacher: *(to calm down the class)* Order, please!
Student: I'll have a root-beer float.

Student: Can you write in the dark?
Father: I think so.
Student: Good, close your eyes and sign my
    report card.

How do you spell sneeze?
    H–U!